STORY VISION®

nickelodeon

SpongeBob SQUAREPANTS

Book & DVD

THE GREAT SNAIL RACE
SPONGEBOB GOES TO THE DOCTOR
HOORAY FOR DADS
BEHOLD, NO CAVITIES!

READ

Have fun reading the story with your child.

WATCH

Watch the animated book on DVD and let the storyteller read to your child as the words appear on screen.

LEARN

Your child can learn to read at their own pace, choosing when to turn the pages of the book and the DVD, and reading along with the animated story.

With Story Vision, you can choose the best way for your child to learn and have fun. Simply select one of the following viewing options:

Option 1

Play the animated book on DVD and let the storyteller read to your child.

Option 2

Let your child choose when to turn the pages of the animated book on DVD and have the storyteller read to them at their own pace.

The Great Snail Race

hinkler

adapted by Kim Ostrow
illustrated by Clint Bond and Andy Clark
based on the teleplay *The Great Snail Race* by Paul Tibbitt, Kent Osborne, and Merriwether Williams

It was a sunny morning in Bikini Bottom. A mailman knocked on Squidward's front door.

"It's finally here," said Squidward.

The mailman glanced at Squidward's signature. "Thank you, Mister . . . mmmmm . . . Tennis Balls."

"That's Tentacles!" corrected Squidward.

"Hey, check out Squidward's new snail," said Patrick.

"Looks like Gary has a new playmate," said SpongeBob.

Squidward rolled his eyes. "I wouldn't let Snellie play with your mongrel mutt. Snellie's a pedigree. Excuse us. She has to train for Bikini Bottom's Snail Race. She'll be winning this Sunday."

4

"Well, I guess I can't enter Gary," said SpongeBob. "Sunday's laundry day!" Squidward sighed. "You can't enter Gary because Gary isn't a purebred! But Snellie has papers!" he said, as he shoved his fancy document toward SpongeBob.

CERTIFICATE OF PEDIGREE
Snellie
PROPERTY OF SQUIDWARD TENTACLES

5

"Patrick, you know what I should do," said SpongeBob.
"I should enter Gary in that race and beat Squidward's snail."

SpongeBob had a lot of work to do. First, he made a nutritional smoothie. Gary took one look at the drink and slithered away.

Patrick came over to show SpongeBob his new snail.
"Your snail is a rock," said SpongeBob.
"He's got nerves of steel," said Patrick proudly.
SpongeBob realized the competition was getting fierce.

SpongeBob blew his whistle. "Let's start with some sprints. On your mark, get set, go!"

Gary barely moved.

"Come on, Gary!" shouted SpongeBob. "You've gotta start training if you're going to win." Just then Squidward peeked in.

"Don't waste your breath, SpongeBob," Squidward said.

"All right, Gary, no more fooling around," instructed SpongeBob. "Come on, move it! Up, up, up! Down, down, down! Faster, faster, faster! Go, go, go!"

The day of the race finally arrived.

"Well, SpongeBob, I didn't think your mongrel mutt would even find the starting line," snickered Squidward.

"Gary happens to be in the best shape of his life," said SpongeBob.

Gary coughed and wheezed.

SpongeBob gave Gary his final pep talk. "Listen up. You're the undersnail. Now, get out there and win!"

"Meow," muttered Gary.

"On your mark!" shouted the referee. "Get set! Slither!"

"And they're off," said the announcer. "Number six, Snellie, rockets out into the lead."

"Go, Snellie! You got it, baby!" cheered Squidward.

Gary hadn't moved.

"What are you doing, Gary?" shouted SpongeBob. "The race has started. Let's go!"

Patrick's snail was also at the starting line. "It's okay, Rocky," Patrick said. "You go when you feel like it."

Go, Gary!

6

Gary panted heavily as he slowly began to move.
"Not good enough!" shouted his coach. "Faster!"

The more SpongeBob yelled, the faster Gary tried to go.
But it was no use. Gary was exhausted.

Suddenly, Gary's bloodshot eye popped!
"It looks like number seven has a blowout," said the announcer.
Shortly after, Gary's other eye blew.

"Make that two, folks," said the announcer.

Gary began to spin out of control and headed straight for the wall! BAM!

"Nooooooo!" shouted SpongeBob. "Hold on, Gary, I'm coming!"

SpongeBob raced to Gary's side.

"One of the coaches has raced onto the track. That is an automatic disqualification. Looks like number six has this race won," said the announcer.

Squidward cheered. "Come on, Snellie."

"Oh, Gary," cried SpongeBob. "Why didn't you say I was pushing you too hard?"

"Meow," said Gary.

"You did? Oh, Gary!" wailed SpongeBob.

Suddenly, Snellie stopped racing. She turned to look at Gary and rushed to his side. The two snails looked into each other's eyes and purred.

"My oh my, folks," said the announcer. "I've never seen anything quite like it."

"Looks like you and me are in-laws. Eh, Squidward?" said SpongeBob.

The crowd cheered as the winner crossed the finish line.
"But that's impossible," said Squidward. "If Snellie didn't win, then who did?"
"And the winner is Rocky," shouted the announcer.
The crowd went wild! Patrick laughed until he cried.

Patrick rushed over. "Don't worry, Squidward. I know how much you wanted to win, so I had the trophy engraved to you."

"Gosh, Patrick, thanks!" He read the plaque out loud. "The snail racing cup is presented to Squidward *Tortellini*."

Patrick and SpongeBob happily hugged their friend.

"It's Squidward Tentacles. Will I ever win?" grumbled Squidward.

SQUIDWARD
TORTELLINI

24

SpongeBob Goes to the Doctor

by Steven Banks
based on a teleplay written by Paul Tibbitt, Ennio Torresan Jr., and Mr. Lawrence
illustrated by Zina Saunders

SpongeBob woke up one morning feeling terrible. When he sneezed, pink bubbles blew out of all his holes.

"Meow," said Gary.

"Don't be silly, Gary," said SpongeBob. "I don't get colds, I get the suds."

27

"Meow," Gary replied.

"No! I can't get the suds!" cried SpongeBob. "I can't miss a day of working at the Krusty Krab!"

"SpongeBob, what's holding up those Krabby Patties?" yelled Mr. Krabs. "What's wrong with you, boy? You're paler than a baby sea horse! Do you have the suds?"

"No, sir!" said SpongeBob weakly. "I feel great! AH . . . AH . . . AH-CHOO!"

"SpongeBob, you're too sick to work," said Mr. Krabs. "Go home and get some rest."

"Who am I kidding, Gary? I've got the suds," said SpongeBob sadly. "I'd better go see the doctor."

SpongeBob called up his friend Sandy Cheeks. "Sandy, I'm sick. Can you take me to the doctor?"

"Sure, SpongeBob!" said Sandy.

"Hey, SpongeBob. Going skiing?" asked Patrick.

"I'm sick, Patrick," said SpongeBob, sniffling. "I'm going to the doctor."

"No!" cried Patrick. "You can't go to the doctor! It's a horrible place!"

"It can't be as horrible as the . . . AH-CHOO! . . . suds," said SpongeBob.
"Yes, it is," said Patrick. "First they make you sit in the . . . *waiting room!*"

"And it gets worse! They make you read … *old magazines!*" said Patrick.
"Oh, no!" cried SpongeBob. "I'm scared. I don't want to go to the doctor!"

"You've got to help me get better, Patrick," said SpongeBob. "Will you be my doctor?"

"Well, I didn't go to doctor school, but sure! I'll do it!" Patrick started putting corks into all of SpongeBob's holes. "There. That ought to do the trick!"

"Do you feel better now, SpongeBob?" asked Patrick.

"I . . . I . . . AH . . . AH . . . AH-CHOO!" SpongeBob sneezed, and he blew up like a balloon. "No bubbles!" said SpongeBob excitedly. "Dr. Patrick, it looks like your treatment is working!"

"I should tell Sandy she doesn't need to take me to the doctor," said SpongeBob.

He tried to push the buttons on the phone, but his fingers were too big and puffy. "Dr. Patrick, will you call Sandy for me?" he asked.

"Hello, Sandy, this is Dr. Patrick. I'm calling on behalf of my patient, Mr. SquarePants. You don't need to take him to the doctor."

"Patrick, you're not a doctor!" said Sandy.

"Sandy's coming anyway," cried Patrick.

"You've got to make me well or she'll take me to the doctor!" yelled SpongeBob.

"I know exactly what to do," said Patrick. He put a giant bandage on SpongeBob's nose, spread jellyfish jelly on his feet, and played a song on the accordion. "Do you feel better?" he asked.

"No!" said SpongeBob.

Sandy pounded on SpongeBob's door. "Open up!" she yelled.
"I'm sorry. There's nobody home," called Patrick.

Sandy karate-chopped the door down. "Patrick, I am taking SpongeBob to see a real doctor!" She pushed SpongeBob out the door and rolled him down the road.

SpongeBob started rolling down the hill toward the Krusty Krab!

"SpongeBob, stop!" shouted Mr. Krabs. "You can't come back to work! You're still sick."

SpongeBob rolled up to the front door and sneezed a giant sneeze.

There was no denying it. SpongeBob needed a *real* doctor.
He went to see the best doctor in Bikini Bottom.
"Well, Mr. SquarePants, you have the suds," said the doctor.

"Are you going to make me wait in the waiting room and read old magazines?" asked a worried SpongeBob.

The doctor laughed. "No, silly. I'll give you some medicine, and you'll feel all better!"

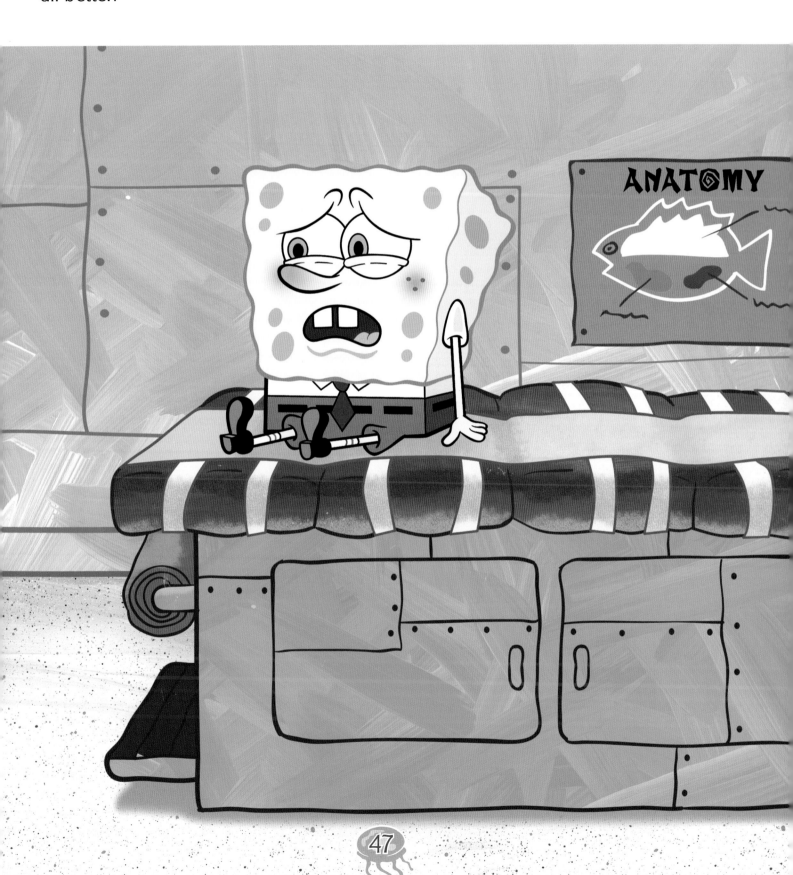

Patrick and Sandy were waiting for SpongeBob in the waiting room.

"SpongeBob, you're all better!" said Sandy.

"I sure am!" said SpongeBob. "Hey, Patrick. Are you enjoying that old magazine you're reading?"

Patrick screamed, "Old magazine! NOOOOOOO!" And he ran away as fast as he could!

HOORAY FOR DADS!

by Erica Pass
illustrated by The Artifact Group

"H[...]ey, Gary, guess what?" said SpongeBob one morning. "Today's the annual Dad[...] and Kid Games Day at Mussel Beach."

"Meow?" asked Gary.

"[...]t's a whole day for dads and their kids to play games and have fun together," said [...] SpongeBob. "And my dad's coming!"

Almost all of Bikini Bottom was at the beach.
"Squidward, are you excited?" asked SpongeBob.
"Thrilled," said Squidward.
"Patrick, are you excited?" asked SpongeBob.

"Yes," said Patrick. "I love the beach!"

"Mr. Krabs, are you excited?" SpongeBob asked.

"I just want to win the grand prize," said Mr. Krabs.

"There's a prize?" asked SpongeBob.

"Of course," said Sandy. "This is a contest. But the prize is a surprise."

"I hope it's a trip to take me far away from here," Squidward said.

"I don't care about the prize," said SpongeBob. "I'm just excited to be with my dad."

Then a bus filled with dads arrived.

"Hooray for dads!" SpongeBob called out.

"Dad!" yelled SpongeBob. "It's so good to see you!"

"You too, son," said SpongeBob's dad.

"Howdy, Sandy!" said Sandy's dad.

"Pearl, let's win that prize!" said Mr. Krabs.

"Uh, yeah, sure, Dad," replied Pearl.

"Hello, Squidward," said Squidward's dad. "At least it's not raining."

"Isn't this a glorious day?" said Plankton's dad.

"Patrick," said Patrick's dad. "The beach!"

"I love the beach!" yelled Patrick.

"Gather around, everyone," said Kip Kelp. "Welcome to our annual Dad and Kid Games Day. It's sure to be great fun."

"Yeah, yeah, yeah," said Squidward. "Get to the good stuff."

"There will be many contests today," continued Kip, "and at the end we have a very special prize for the best team."

"Hear that, Pearl?" Mr. Krabs said. "That prize is ours!"

"Just please don't embarrass me!" said Pearl.

The first competition was a relay race, which Sandy and her dad won.
"Dad, we're on our way to winning that prize!" said Sandy.
"Sandy," said SpongeBob, "there are more important things than winning."

Next was a competition to see which team could blow the most bubbles.

"My Pearl is an expert bubble-blower!" said Mr. Krabs.

SpongeBob and his dad blew beautiful bubbles, not caring how many there were.

Squidward and his dad blew the most bubbles. "Prize, here I come!" Squidward called out.

"Not so fast, Squid," said Sandy. "You haven't won yet."

Next the teams had to build sand castles. Squidward hurried to build a tall tower—but it crashed down.

"You'd better calm down," Sandy said to Squidward, "or that prize is mine!"

SpongeBob was all set for rounding up the jellyfish. "Jellyfish love me!" he said to his dad. "And I love them!"

SpongeBob and his dad soon gathered the most jellyfish.

"Nice work, SpongeBob," said Sandy.

"Hey SpongeBob," said Squidward. "I heard the grand prize is something you've been wanting for a while . . ."

"You heard it's a gold-plated spatula?" asked SpongeBob.

"Oh, Dad," said SpongeBob. "I've wanted a gold-plated spatula forever! We must win."

"But I thought today was all about spending time with the people you love," said his dad.

"And I love spatulas. Let's go!" said SpongeBob.

Next was a badminton tournament, and SpongeBob tried hard to win, running circles around his dad.

"Out of my way!" SpongeBob yelled.

"There are more important things than winning," said SpongeBob's dad.

"Of course there are," SpongeBob replied. "Like what I can do with that golden spatula!"

SpongeBob's dad sighed.

There were many more contests, and by the end of the day everyone was tired out. Finally Kip Kelp announced the winner of the grand prize.

"This has been an inspiring Dad and Kid Games Day," said Kip. "The winning team is … Plankton and his dad!"

Plankton hopped up onto the stage, excited. "What did we win?" he asked.

"You've won the honor of having your names inscribed on a plaque in the middle of town," said Kip.

"Uh … that's it?" asked Plankton. "I ran around in circles all day long for this?"

Hearing Plankton's words, SpongeBob turned to his dad. "I'm sorry," he said. "I lost sight of what it means to be able to spend time with you."

"That's all right, SpongeBob," said his dad. "We all want to win sometimes. But I had a great time just being with you."

"Yeah, me too, Dad," said SpongeBob.

"Everyone is welcome to come to the Krusty Krab," Mr. Krabs announced.

"Woo-hoo!" said SpongeBob. "Dad, who needs a gold-plated spatula when I have you?"

BEHOLD, No CAVITIES!

by Sarah Wilson
illustrated by Harry Moore

"Today is the day! It's finally here!" said SpongeBob as he bounded out of bed.

"Meow!" said Gary.

"That's right, Gary. It *has* been exactly six months, two hours, and seven minutes since my last dental cleaning. So today I get to go again!"

SpongeBob raced off to brush his teeth.

Patrick came to visit while SpongeBob was still brushing.
"SpongeBob! What's wrong? You're foaming at the mouth!" he cried
in alarm.

"Ish jusht tooshpashte, shilly," said SpongeBob, spitting out the toothpaste and showing Patrick his dazzling smile.

"Oh! I always wondered what that thing was," said Patrick, pointing at SpongeBob's toothbrush.

SpongeBob's mouth dropped open. "You don't floss or brush your teeth, Patrick?"

"Nope."

"Have you *ever* been to a dentist?"

"What's a dentist?"

"Patrick, ol' buddy," he said. "I think you had better come along with me to see my dentist, Dr. Gill, today."

"Will it be scary?" Patrick asked, clutching onto SpongeBob.

SpongeBob smiled. "No, Patrick. Dr. Gill's office is the friendliest place in the world. And I am their best patient. Everyone here knows me!"

He threw open the door.

"Hello! And who are you, young man?" asked the receptionist.
"I thought everyone here knew you," whispered Patrick.
"She must be new," SpongeBob whispered back.

"SpongeBob! You're here!" shrieked a voice.

"Hi, Debbie!" called SpongeBob. "Debbie is the person who cleans your teeth. And Dr. Gill makes sure you don't have any cavities, but if you do he'll fix them."

Debbie and Dr. Gill joined hands with SpongeBob and sang their dental cleaning song:
"I brush and floss my teeth each day
To ward away that tooth decay!"

"Gee," said Patrick. "I had no idea getting your teeth cleaned could be fun."
"Oh, Patrick," said SpongeBob. "You haven't seen *anything* yet! Behold the No Cavi-Tree!"

"Wow. Why is it full of teeth that say 'SpongeBob'?" asked Patrick.
"Because you get your name added when you have no cavities at your checkup!" SpongeBob replied.

"Time for your cleaning, SpongeBob!" called Debbie cheerfully. "First, let's take a new X-ray."

Next Debbie cleaned SpongeBob's teeth, polished them, rinsed them, and suctioned the water out of his mouth with Mr. Thirsty.

Then Dr. Gill had a look. "We won't know for sure until we see the X-rays, but your teeth look very healthy," he said.

"Thanks, Dr. Gill," said SpongeBob. "Now it's time to look at my friend Patrick's teeth."

Patrick got in the chair and opened his mouth. Debbie and Dr. Gill took turns peering in. Dr. Gill buzzed the receptionist. "Cancel the rest of the appointments today," he said. "This will take awhile."

Finally Patrick's teeth were clean.

"You boys go home and I'll call you both tomorrow with the results of your X-rays," called Dr. Gill.

The next morning Patrick burst into SpongeBob's house. "No cavities!" he yelled. "I get to have my name on the No Cavi-Tree!"

"Patrick! That's great!" said SpongeBob.

BRIIIING!

SpongeBob answered his phone. "Yes, this is SpongeBob. I . . . I . . . what? Okay. I'll be there at two o'clock. Buh-buh-buh-bye." SpongeBob hung up the phone and burst into tears. "I have four cavities!" he sobbed.
"I'll come with you to get them filled, old buddy," Patrick said.

"Hello again, SpongeBob and Patrick," said Dr. Gill that afternoon. He looked at SpongeBob's X-rays. "It seems you have . . . wait. These aren't *your* X-rays!"

"They're not?" asked SpongeBob.

"No! These are Patrick's! My receptionist must have mixed them up!"

"I HAVE NO CAVITIES!" SpongeBob cried, leaping out of the chair.
"Woo-hoo! Way to go, SpongeBob!" shouted Patrick joyfully. Everyone
linked arms and danced merrily. Suddenly Patrick stopped dancing. "But that
means *I* have cavities."

Debbie patted the chair. "Hop up, Patrick," she said kindly. "Dr. Gill will have these filled in a jiffy."

"It didn't hurt a bit!" Patrick said when Dr. Gill had finished.

"Now remember, Patrick," said Dr. Gill. "Floss your teeth every night. Brush them twice a day. And come back to see me every six months! Now go pick a new toothbrush from the drawer!"

Patrick and SpongeBob watched the receptionist pin another "SpongeBob" tooth on the No Cavi-Tree. "Next time I come I want to see my name up on the No Cavi-Tree!" said Patrick.

"I'm sure you will, Patrick," said SpongeBob.